Paddington
at the
Circus

First published in hardback by HarperCollins Publishers, USA, in 2000
First published in hardback in Great Britain by Collins in 2000
First published in paperback by Collins in 2001
This edition published by HarperCollins Children's Books in 2016

3 5 7 9 10 8 6 4 2

ISBN: 978-0-00-817366-1

Collins in an imprint of HarperCollins Publishers Ltd.
HarperCollins Children's Books is a division of HarperCollins Publishers Ltd.

Text copyright © Michael Bond 2000
Illustrations copyright © R. W. Alley 2000

Visit our website at www.harpercollins.co.uk

Printed in China

MIX
Paper from
responsible sources
FSC® C007454

FSC is a non-profit international organisation established to promote the
responsible management of the world's forests. Products carrying the FSC
label are independently certified to assure consumers that they come
from forests that are managed to meet the social, economic and
ecological needs of present and future generations.

Find out more about HarperCollins and the environment at
www.harpercollins.co.uk/green

Michael Bond
Paddington
at the
Circus

Illustrated by R. W. Alley

HarperCollins *Children's Books*

One morning Paddington was doing his shopping in the market when he saw a very tall man with a pointed hat and baggy trousers.

The man was putting up a poster, and he was so tall, he didn't even need a ladder to reach the top of the billboard.

The poster showed a huge tent decorated with coloured lights, and across the middle were the words SEE THE WORLD'S GREATEST CIRCUS! ONE NIGHT ONLY.

Paddington rubbed his eyes several times in order to make sure he wasn't dreaming.

Paddington hurried back home to tell the others what he had seen.

"The world's greatest circus?" repeated Jonathan, giving his sister a wink. "Are you sure?"

"It's for one night only!" exclaimed Paddington.

"Don't worry," said Judy. "You won't miss it."

"Dad's got tickets for the front row," added Jonathan. "Mrs Bird's coming, too."

Paddington had never been to a circus before, and he was very excited at the thought. "I hope it gets dark early," he said. "Then we can see the lights."

Paddington's wish came true. Seen from the outside, with all the coloured lights twinkling against the night sky, the circus really did have a magical air.

"Hurry! Hurry! Have your tickets ready!" called a voice. "The show's about to begin."

"It's the man I saw this morning," whispered Paddington. "The very tall one I was telling you about."

"That's one of the clowns," said Judy.

"He isn't really that tall…" began Jonathan. But Paddington couldn't wait. He could hear a band playing, and he was already hurrying on ahead.

But if the outside of the tent had seemed exciting,
it was nothing compared to the inside.

There was a lovely smell of sawdust, and in
amongst the jugglers and the acrobats there
was even a girl selling ice cream.

Mr Brown pointed to a man in the middle
of the ring. He was wearing a top hat.

"That's the ringmaster," he explained.
"He's in charge of everything."

"I expect you could keep a lot
of marmalade sandwiches under a hat
like that," said Paddington enviously.
"I think I would like to be
a ringmaster one day."

Just then the tall clown entered the ring. He was clutching a long pole that had a bucket balanced on the end of it. When he saw Paddington waving, he came across to greet him.

"Watch out!" cried Jonathan, as the clown leaned over to shake Paddington's paw.

Paddington jumped up in alarm. But he wasn't quick enough. Before he had time to escape, the bucket had fallen off the end of the pole.

Luckily, it was tied on
with string and it was
empty, so Paddington
didn't get wet.

"Clowns are full of tricks,"
said Judy.

"I'm glad I was wearing my
duffle coat all the same,"
said Paddington.

"Someone might have
put water in the bucket
by mistake."

"I'm told ice cream is very good for young bears if they've had
a shock," said Mr Brown.

He ordered six large cones, then they all sat back to enjoy the show.

"I feel better already, Mr Brown," said Paddington gratefully.

Paddington had hardly started on his ice
cream when he had yet another shock.
Glancing up towards the roof of the tent,
he saw a man hanging from a rope.
Jonathan looked at his programme.
"That must be one of the Popular Prices,"
he said. "They're trapeze artists."
"Don't worry!" called Paddington.
"I'm coming. Bears are good at climbing."

Before the others could stop him, Paddington
was halfway up the nearest tent pole.
Climbing the pole and carrying an ice
cream at the same time wasn't easy, and
the audience gave a round of applause
when he reached the safety of a
small platform near the top.

Paddington was about to take a bow, when to his surprise
he saw a man coming towards him on a bicycle.

"I don't think you're supposed to bring your bicycle
up here, Mr Price!" he exclaimed.

"Look out!" shouted the man,
frantically ringing his bell. "I can't stop!"
"Hold on!" called his partner.

In the confusion, Paddington didn't know which to do first,
so he grabbed hold of a nearby bar.

It came away in his paw, and before he knew what
was happening, he felt himself flying through the air.

The audience thought Paddington was
part of the act, and they clapped
louder than ever.

Then a gasp went up as he missed
the platform on the other
side of the tent and began
swinging backwards
and forwards in midair.

"Oh, dear!" said Mrs Brown. "Whatever will he do now?"

"I shouldn't worry," said Mrs Bird. "Bears usually land on their feet."

But even Mrs Bird went quiet as Paddington's swings got slower and
slower, until finally he ended up hanging over the middle of the ring.

"Don't let go!" shouted the ringmaster. "Whatever you do – don't let go!"

"I'm not going to!" cried Paddington.

He tried to raise his hat, but he was still holding the ice cream cone in his other paw.

A look of horror came over the ringmaster's face as something soft and white landed with a squelch on his beautifully clean top hat.

"Help!" cried Paddington. "I've changed my mind. I can't hold on much longer."

Everybody in the audience began making suggestions, but in the end it was the clown who came to the rescue. Balancing his bucket on the end of the pole, he stretched up as high as he could so that Paddington could climb into it.

"I hope the string doesn't break," said Mrs Bird. "That bear had a very large lunch."

"If the clown stretches any more," said Judy, "his trousers will fall down."

Sure enough they did, and the cheers changed
to laughter as Paddington was lowered to safety.

"Funniest act I've seen in years!" shouted a man near the Browns. "More! More!"

Paddington gave the man a hard stare. "I don't think I want to do any more," he announced. "In fact, I don't think I want to go on a trapeze ever again. I shall just sit and watch from now on."

Then he caught sight of the clown's stilts. "It's no wonder you look so tall!" he exclaimed.

Paddington didn't think anything more *could* happen to him, but at the end of the evening the ringmaster presented him with another ice cream and insisted he take part in the Grand Parade.

"After all," he said, "you *were* the star of the show."

"It's a pity we are moving on," he added, turning to the Browns. "It isn't every evening we have a daring young bear on the flying trapeze."

"If you ask me," said Mrs Bird wisely, "it's a good thing you don't. Otherwise there's no knowing where you would end up."

Later that evening, when the Browns said good night to
Paddington, they found him standing on the box seat by his
bedroom window. He had a faraway look in his eyes.

"I was taking a last look at the circus before it goes on
its way," he explained.

"Do you still want to be a ringmaster
one day?" asked Judy.

Paddington climbed into bed and tested his sheets carefully to make sure he was safely tucked in before answering. Then he lay back.

"I think perhaps I would sooner be a clown," he said dreamily. "It must be nice to be so tall. You can always see what's going on in the world without having to stand on anything."